To all the New Someones. May kindness always be stronger than fear,
and may you be welcomed with open paws. —J.T.

For Richard —EG.K.

The Someone New • Text copyright © 2019 by Jill Twiss • Illustrations copyright © 2019 by EG Keller. • All rights reserved. Printed in the United States of America. • No part of this book may be used or reproduced in any manner whatsoever without written permission except in the case of brief quotations embodied in critical articles and reviews. For information address HarperCollins Children's Books, a division of HarperCollins Publishers, 195 Broadway, New York, NY 10007. • www.harpercollinschildrens.com • Library of Congress Control Number: 2018964867 • ISBN 978-0-06-293374-4 • The artist created the illustrations for this book digitally. Design by Chelsea C. Donaldson • 19 20 21 22 23 PC 10 9 8 7 6 5 4 3 2 1 ❖ First Edition

THE
SOMEONE
NEW

Written by Jill Twiss   Illustrated by EG Keller

HARPER
An Imprint of HarperCollinsPublishers

When Jitterbug woke up, she could already tell: Something was New.

Jitterbug was a careful chipmunk. She liked it when things stayed the Same.

When Something was New she got a little quiver in her tummy.

"What is this Something New?" she wondered. "Is it Toast the butterfly? No! She is flitting from flower to flower, sharing her Important Thoughts like every other day."

"Hello hello hello!" shouted Jitterbug.
"Hello, Jitterbug!" said Toast. "Did you know that a group of butterflies is called a kaleidoscope?"

Whoa. That was good information. But it was not
the Something New. Jitterbug kept looking.

"Is it Geezer the goose or Duffles and Nudge the otters?" she wondered. "No! They are splashing in the river just like always."

"Hello hello hello!" shouted Jitterbug.

"Honk honk HONK," said Geezer, who sounded grouchy even when he wasn't.

"Good day to you, Jitterbug!" said Duffles.

"Didja hear the thunderstorm last night? It just—" said Nudge.

"—missed our forest," said Duffles.

Whoa. That was good information. But Duffles and Nudge were best friends; they always finished each other's thoughts. That was not the Something New.

Then Jitterbug saw Something she had never seen before.

It was both hard and soft. It was both round and *even more round*. It was Something New.

No, wait. It was Some*one* New. And that Someone New was moving toward them verrrrryyyyy sllooowwwwwlly.

"Hellohellohello?" Jitterbug said nervously. Jitterbug's tummy was doing some pretty-big-time tummy quivers.

"Hellooooo!" said the Someone. "My name is Pudding."

"Hello, Pudding!" said Toast. "Did you know that butterflies taste with their feet?"

"Hello and how do you do?" said Nudge.

"Excuse us for asking—" said Duffles.

"—but what exactly *are* you?" whispered Nudge.

After a long pause, Pudding said, "I am a snail. I am from the garden over the big hill."

Whoa. That was good information. Jitterbug had never seen a snail before. A snail was definitely Someone New.

"Why did you leave your garden and come here?" asked Jitterbug.

Pudding did not answer right away. If there was one thing Jitterbug had learned about snails—and so far there was only one thing Jitterbug had learned about snails—it was that they answered questions verrrrrryyyyyy slllloooooowwwwwlllyy.

Pudding took a breath. "Last night, there was a big storm and my garden flooded. Everything around me washed away, and I was left all alone. I squished all the way here to be safe. I want to stay here."

"With us?" said Jitterbug cautiously. "In our forest?"

Pudding nodded.

"But but but!" said Jitterbug, thinking aloud. "But what if there are not enough acorns for all of us? What if everyone decides that squishy snails like Pudding are nicer than furry chipmunks like me?"

"What if everything is . . .
DIFFERENT?"

Jitterbug's tummy quivers were turning
into tummy cartwheels.

Pudding had just opened his mouth to
answer when—

"Pudding, I am very sorry for your home, but you cannot stay here," Jitterbug blurted out.

Pudding looked at Jitterbug, looked back toward his old garden, and then quietly began to squish back the way he'd come. Everything was going to stay the Same. Jitterbug's tummy relaxed until . . .

She looked up and saw her friends.
"What what what?" said Jitterbug.

"Did you know that I was New once?" spluttered Toast. "I used to be a caterpillar!"

"Honk honk HONK. I was also New once," said Geezer. "I used to live in a beautiful lake. Then people started to fill it with garbage until it wasn't safe for me anymore. That's when I came here."

"You were both New?" said Jitterbug. "It feels like you all have always been beside me, honking your honks and flitting around our flowers."

"That is how friends feel," said Duffles.
"Even when they are New, friends feel like
you've known them forever," said Nudge.
"But New can be scary!" said Jitterbug.

"Jitterbug, do you remember when Toast wanted to see her reflection, so she flew very close to the river?" asked Geezer.

"Oh yes," said Jitterbug. "Toast flew so close to the river that pretty soon she had flown *into* the river!"

"No one else was around—" said Nudge.

"—and you had always been so scared of swimming," said Duffles.

"But even though you were frightened," said Geezer, "you jumped right into the water and saved Toast. Because even though New *can* be scary, kindness is stronger than fear."

Whoa. That was *very* good information. "I have to go get Pudding!" yelped Jitterbug.

Jitterbug ran as fast as she could, and when she thought she had looked everywhere . . .

. . . she found Pudding right around the corner.

If there was one thing Jitterbug had learned about snails—and so far there was *still* only one thing Jitterbug had learned about snails—it was that they ran away verrrryyyy slloooowwllly.

"Pudding," said Jitterbug, "I was wrong! Please please please come live with us! I was scared because you are New. But then I realized how scared you must be in a place where *everyone* is New. You were so brave to come here. Let's be scared together."

"Thank you, Jitterbug. I will miss my old home,
but now I can make a new one with all of you."

And Pudding stayed.

Because kindness *is* stronger than fear.

(And sometimes it takes very special friends
to be brave enough to tell you you are wrong.)

Pretty soon it felt like Pudding had
been there Forever.

Now there were many things Jitterbug knew about snails—she knew that they were strong and brave and smart and kind. . . .

But if there was one thing Jitterbug knew about snails,
it was that they are Very Good Friends.